Dear Parents:

Congratulations! Your child is taking the first steps on an exciting journey. The destination? Independent reading!

STEP INTO READING® will help your child get there. The program offers five steps to reading success. Each step includes fun stories and colorful art or photographs. In addition to original fiction and books with favorite characters, there are Step into Reading Non-Fiction Readers, Phonics Readers and Boxed Sets, Sticker Readers, and Comic Readers—a complete literacy program with something to interest every child.

Learning to Read, Step by Step!

Ready to Read Preschool–Kindergarten
• big type and easy words • rhyme and rhythm • picture clues
For children who know the alphabet and are eager to begin reading.

Reading with Help Preschool–Grade 1
• basic vocabulary • short sentences • simple stories
For children who recognize familiar words and sound out new words with help.

Reading on Your Own Grades 1–3
• engaging characters • easy-to-follow plots • popular topics
For children who are ready to read on their own.

Reading Paragraphs Grades 2–3
• challenging vocabulary • short paragraphs • exciting stories
For newly independent readers who read simple sentences with confidence.

Ready for Chapters Grades 2–4
• chapters • longer paragraphs • full-color art
For children who want to take the plunge into chapter books but still like colorful pictures.

STEP INTO READING® is designed to give every child a successful reading experience. The grade levels are only guides; children will progress through the steps at their own speed, developing confidence in their reading.

Remember, a lifetime love of reading starts with a single step!

Special thanks to Alex Wiltshire, Sherin Kwan, Jay Castello, Kelsey Ranallo, and Milo Bengtsson

All rights reserved. Published in the United States by Random House Children's Books, a division of Penguin Random House LLC, 1745 Broadway, New York, NY 10019, and in Canada by Penguin Random House Canada Limited, Toronto.

Step into Reading, Random House, and the Random House colophon are registered trademarks of Penguin Random House LLC.

Visit us on the Web!
rhcbooks.com
minecraft.net

Educators and librarians, for a variety of teaching tools, visit us at RHTeachersLibrarians.com

ISBN 978-0-593-70990-0 (trade) — ISBN 978-0-593-70991-7 (lib. bdg.)
ISBN 978-0-593-70992-4 (ebook)

Printed in the United States of America
10 9 8 7 6 5 4 3 2 1

MINECRAFT

TROUBLE BREWING!

by Arie Kaplan

illustrated by Alan Batson

Random House 🏠 New York

Emmy and Birch had just returned from the Nether.

They had collected some Nether wart, two golden carrots, and a brown mushroom.

4

Before the portal took them home,
the duo battled some blazes!

It was a hard fight,
but they managed to win.
Emmy even picked up
a few blaze rods!

Back in the Overworld,
the three friends found
a tall cliff.
"I'll mine some stone,"
Emmy said.
"We'll need cobblestone and wood
to make a crafting table!"

6

Birch went to get some wood
from a nearby tree.

Using her pickaxe,
Emmy mined the cliff.
Soon she had several
blocks of cobblestone!

Meanwhile,
Birch punched the tree.
It broke apart
into blocks of wood.

HHIIIISS!

Just then,
a creeper slid by.

9

The creeper
was ready to explode!
Birch and Emmy
defeated it just in time!
The creeper left behind
a small pile of gray powder.

"Look," Emmy said,

pointing to the pile.

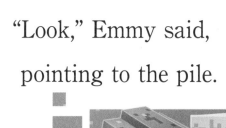

"The creeper dropped

some gunpowder!"

But as Birch bent down

to scoop up the pile . . .

The gravel under them
gave way!
Our heroes fell
to the bottom
of a deep ravine.

It was so dark
it was hard to see!

The three friends heard the sounds of witches, skeletons, and zombies approaching. "That's no surprise," Birch said. "Hostile mobs spawn in dark places like this."

The hostile mobs got louder
as they came closer.
"Too bad we don't
have any torches!" Emmy added.
"Then we could *see* the mobs!"

Suddenly, Emmy had an idea.

With Birch standing guard,
she crafted a brewing stand
with a blaze rod and cobblestone.
The other rod became blaze powder
to power the brewing stand!

Using the Nether wart
and two water bottles,
she made two awkward potions.

Combining those with
two golden carrots,
Emmy brewed
two potions of Night Vision!

Emmy gave one of the potions
to Birch
and drank the other.
Now she could
see perfectly!

"There you are!"
Emmy said to the
hostile mobs.

The witches just laughed
at them!

The witches

tossed potions at Emmy.

She ducked to avoid getting hit.

Then she swung her sword.

Soon both of the witches

were defeated.

As one witch fell,

they dropped a spider's eye.

The other witch

dropped some sugar.

Before Emmy could
pick up the dropped loot,
a skeleton and a zombie
came out of nowhere
and lunged at her!

Emmy picked up her sword
to bravely fight off the mobs.
"They just keep coming!"
she said, her arm growing tired.

Suddenly, an invisible force
defeated the skeleton.
What was happening?

"Hi, Emmy,"
the invisible force said.
"It's me, Birch!"

Emmy couldn't believe
what she was hearing.

Using the items
the witches dropped,
Birch had crafted
a fermented spider's eye.

Then he brewed the eye
with the other
potion of Night Vision.

The result was

a potion of Invisibility!

Emmy noticed a block
of coal ore nearby.
Using her pickaxe,
she mined the coal
with lightning speed!

She crafted the coal
and some sticks
into torches.
Emmy's timing was perfect,
because just then,
her potion of Night Vision
wore off!

Moments later,
Birch's potion
wore off as well.
He became visible again.
Birch and Emmy
placed the torches
on the walls of the cave.

With the torches
lighting the way,
the friends found their way
out of the cave quickly!

Emmy and Birch
took the brewing stand home.
Using some sugar,
they brewed
potions of Swiftness,
then raced each other
until the end of the day!